GAME FACE

No Relief

by Rich Wallace
illustrated by Tim Heitz

Calico

An Imprint of Magic Wagon
abdopublishing.com

abdopublishing.com

Printed in the United States of America, North Mankato, Minnesota.
092015
012016

 **THIS BOOK CONTAINS RECYCLED MATERIALS**

Written by Rich Wallace
Illustrated by Tim Heitz
Edited by Heidi M.D. Elston, Megan M. Gunderson & Bridget O'Brien
Designed by Laura Mitchell

Extra special thanks to our content consultant, Scott Lauinger!

Library of Congress Cataloging-in-Publication Data

Wallace, Rich, author.
  No relief / by Rich Wallace ; illustrated by Tim Heitz.
     pages cm. -- (Game face)
  Summary: Seventh-grader Javon is the relief pitcher for his summer league baseball team and they are in the championship tournament--trouble is there is one player on the team they are playing that he cannot seem to get out.
  ISBN 978-1-62402-134-3 (alk. paper)
1. Baseball stories. 2. Pitching (Baseball)--Juvenile fiction. 3. Relief pitchers (Baseball)--Juvenile fiction. 4. Teamwork (Sports)--Juvenile fiction. [1. Baseball--Fiction. 2. Teamwork (Sports)--Fiction.] I. Heitz, Tim, illustrator. II. Title.
  PZ7.W15877No 2016
  813.54--dc23
  [Fic]
                              2015024916

TABLE OF CONTENTS

ONE

Closing the Door

I don't mind the bench. I'm certainly used to it. Last basketball season, I was the shortest guy on the team. I considered myself lucky if I played a few mop-up minutes at the end of a blowout. Mostly I collected splinters on the bench.

Baseball's different. I usually sit for the first three innings. By the fourth, Coach sends me out to center field, like he did today. I can catch. I'm plenty fast enough to chase down deep hits. And I can definitely throw. That's my best asset.

The sixth inning is my time. If we have the lead—and we usually do—I replace the pitcher. I don't have the arm strength to pitch a whole game, but for short bursts I'm tough to hit. Usually that's an inning or less.

The final-inning pitching specialist is called the closer. Or the fireman. Or sometimes just the relief pitcher.

Whatever you call it, I'm the guy who goes in for the save—closing out a win by shutting down the opponent's last chance to score. I've picked up six saves this season, so I'm good at it. Nobody else in the league has more than three.

Of course, I don't always hold the lead. Twice I've wasted it in the final inning and lost the game. Both times it was against the same opponent. But most of the time I'm gold.

Carlos is pitching great today, so I may as well be picking dandelions out here. Trouble is, we haven't been hitting much either. It's 1–1, bottom of the fifth. There's a good chance I'll bat in the sixth. If we get a run, I'll probably pitch after that.

Crack!

The ball streaks on a line drive over the second baseman's head. I'm at full speed in an instant. It looks like the ball will drop between me and the right fielder, but I just . . . might . . . get there!

I dive, reaching out my glove, and the ball lands squarely in the pocket.

Out! Inning over.

"Great grab, Javon!" yells Lamar, yanking me to my feet. The rest of my teammates are yelling, too. I've got a green streak up my leg from sliding on the grass.

Sprinting to the dugout, I pass my friend Marcus, who's on his way to center field for our opponents.

"Lucky catch," he says, grinning.

"You were lucky to witness it," I reply. "That was the play of the year for sure."

I feel tall running next to Lamar. It's nice to have a teammate who's shorter than I am. I've got a half inch on him.

I smack hands with Griffin as I reach the dugout. He's pulling off his shin guards and helmet, since he'll bat third this inning. He's our catcher, so we team up whenever I pitch. I follow him in the batting order, too.

Carlos gives me a fist bump. He's sweating hard from all that work on the mound. His red Pedraza's jersey is soaked through. "Incredible catch," he says, a little out of breath.

"Thanks. How's the arm?"

"Loose, but tired." He shakes it out. "Let's score a run and finish this thing."

"We just need one base runner," I say. "I'll drive him home."

Griffin puts on a batting glove and chooses a bat. He has power, but he's slow on the bases. It's hot behind the plate with all that equipment on, so I know he's itching to get this game over with. We don't want extra innings.

But there's already one out.

Lamar steps to the batter's box and taps the plate. The advantage of being short is that he and I draw a lot of walks. Our strike zone is small.

Four high pitches. Lamar trots to first base.

Everybody in the dugout stands up. Griffin's hit four home runs this season, and he just missed one earlier today.

I'm on deck. I shove a batting helmet over my ears (they stick out of my regular cap) and swing the bat a few times.

Griffin lines the first pitch deep into left-center. Looks like it might be gone, but it dips at the last second and bangs off the fence. Marcus makes a great stab and fires the ball in, holding Lamar at third as Griffin slides into second.

So it's all on me.

"One out, Javon!" Carlos calls.

Another out here is okay, especially if it brings in a run. *Don't strike out,* I tell myself. *Don't hit a weak pop fly or a grounder to first.*

Just do something productive.

"Strike one!" the umpire calls as a fastball zips by me.

I wipe my mouth with the back of my wrist.

"No batter!" call the infielders. "He can't hit."

I don't mind the chatter. I catch the second baseman's eye and smirk. Torry Santana. He and Marcus are the only players in the league with their names on their jerseys. Their fathers sponsor the team, just like Pedraza's Mexican Restaurant sponsors ours: Thorpe & Santana. It's an accounting agency.

"Strike two!" This time I take a swing at least. But I miss it by a mile.

There's a lot on the line here. If we win this game, we'll finish the regular season in a tie for first place. Lose, and the season's over. There'll only be a play-off if the standings are tied.

Here comes the pitch. Waist high, a little outside.

Whack!

I sprint toward first base as the ball soars into the outfield. Marcus is under it, but that might be deep enough to drive Lamar home.

Marcus catches the ball before I reach first base.

I turn and yell to Lamar. "Move, buddy!"

The throw bounces near the mound and the catcher blocks the plate. Lamar slides, stirring up a cloud of dirt.

Safe. We have the lead!

I smack hands with my teammates as I reach the dugout. That was a huge RBI. Maybe a season saver.

Carlos strikes out, so I grab my glove.

"Javon," Coach says. He doesn't need to say anything more. I run to the mound and throw some pitches to an assistant coach while Griffin straps on his catcher's gear. Carlos takes my place in center field.

Then we're ready to go.

"Batter up!" calls the umpire.

I glare at Torry, one of my best friends but an enemy at the moment. He drove in his team's only run a few innings ago.

My first pitch sizzles right past him for a strike. So does the second, as he takes a massive swing.

Bye-bye, Torry, I think as I hurl the ball toward the plate.

Pop!

Such a satisfying sound as the ball lands in Griffin's glove.

"Strike three!" yells the umpire.

Torry never looks back as he drags his bat to the dugout.

The next batter hits a soft fly ball to the shortstop for the second out.

I fan the third guy on three pitches.

Game over. We're in the play-offs! Time for some french fries and a nice cold drink.

And maybe a little gloating. I earned it.

TWO

A Mighty Ant

"I'll buy," I say as we line up at the refreshment stand. My mom gave me some money to treat Griffin, Torry, and Marcus, since this was the last regular-season game. Plus, it's Saturday, so my meal schedule is random.

"All we can eat?" Torry asks.

"No," I reply. "All I can afford. One soda apiece and one food thing. If you want anything more than that you're on your own."

I start with fries and lots of ketchup, and we sit at a picnic table behind the third-base dugout.

"Sorry about making you look bad out there," I say to Torry. I'm sure he can tell by my expression that I don't feel bad at all. He's very athletic and very intense on the playing field. He usually runs circles around me in any sport, so getting the upper hand on him for a change is cool.

I swing at the air as if I'm striking out. "Whoosh, whoosh, whoosh!"

Torry shakes his head and finishes chewing his hot dog. "I've gotta admit, you can definitely put some heat on those pitches."

"And he only weighs about forty pounds," Griffin says.

"Twice that," I say.

Griffin steals one of my fries. "You're like an ant or something, Javon. Aren't they supposed to be a hundred times stronger than humans, pound for pound?"

I shrug. "Ask Torry. He's the scientist." But I flex my biceps and a little muscle pops up.

Torry says he doesn't know the answer. He stands up and says he's getting another hot dog. "This season went way too fast," he says. "Can't believe it's over."

"Over for you," I say. "Now the spotlight's on the elite teams. The best of the best. Us."

I try to act confident around these guys, but I'm usually in awe of what strong athletes they are. Pitching is about the only area of sports where I can match up with them, or even be a little better.

The final standings have already been posted on the wall outside the refreshment stand, so we hustle over to have a look. I know who we'll be playing for the championship: Turn-It-Up Used Records. The team that came from behind to beat us twice this season. Both times I wasted our lead.

Griffin leans in and reads the standings. "Oh, man," he says with a sigh. "We have to play the Turnips again."

"Who?" I ask.

"The Turnips." He points to the top line of the standings.

I shake my head and stare at him for a few seconds. "Turn . . . It . . . Up," I say.

He looks bewildered. "Turn what up?"

"That's the name of the team. Like Bagelworks and Prime Roast and all the other teams. Those are the sponsors. You know that, right?"

"Yeah."

"So why would a team be named the Turnips?" I ask.

He nods, but I'm not sure he gets it.

"What's Turn-It-Up?" he asks.

"Used records and CDs. We pass it every day. It's downstairs under Bagelworks. You never noticed it before?"

Griffin shrugs. "I thought they were called the Turnips. Their jerseys are purple."

Marcus steps between us. "I think Turnips is a great name," he says. "Go Turnips!"

"No," I say. "Go Pedraza's!" Then I think it over. "Beat the Turnips!"

"I think you mash turnips," Torry says. "With butter."

"Sounds awful," I say. "But if it makes us the champions, we can beat 'em, mash 'em, squash 'em, or roast 'em."

I scoop up the last of the ketchup with a very crispy french fry, then crumple the paper dish and shoot it toward a garbage bin. Score!

"Nice shot," Torry says. "Which reminds me, you guys up for some hoops?"

Two-on-two driveway basketball is one of my favorite things to do. But I decline. "I should rest my arm," I reply.

"How tired can it be?" Torry says. "You threw four pitches!"

"Twice that," I say, stretching my pitching arm. "And it's not tired. But I'm not taking any chances. I could throw three days in a row in the play-offs."

"Pool, then," Marcus says. "Your arm can float."

That sounds good. It's hot and getting hotter.

The pool is next to the ball field. Unfortunately, our swimsuits are across town at our houses.

"This is typical of us, huh?" Griffin says. "If we'd planned for half a second this morning, we could have brought our stuff for the pool."

"I was too focused on the game," Torry says. "You know me. I never think beyond that."

So we head for our neighborhood, ten blocks away. Heat is reflecting off the asphalt street.

"Maybe we can get a ride back," I say.

"Don't look at me," Marcus replies. "I can just hear my dad. 'Exercise is good for you. Keep marching!'"

My parents would say the same. But I have an older brother, Ki. He's a little more likely to yield.

There's no car in the driveway when I reach my house. "Anybody home?" I call as I unlock the door.

"How'd it go?" says Ki, running down the stairs.

"Won it. Made the play-offs. Where are Mom and Dad?"

"At the pool."

"You've got to be kidding. I just walked, like, four hours from there."

"On your hands?" Ki jokes. "Sorry I missed the game. We were jamming all morning at Tavo's. We have a gig tonight."

Ki is a drummer, and he's teaching me to play. His band plays at parties sometimes. Nothing big yet. They're all over the place musically. They play hip-hoppy rock stuff with some rap and reggae.

Ki says he's sorting out his musical heritage and influences. Our dad is Korean, and even at his age he listens to K-Pop. Mom grew up listening to Motown with her parents, so we hear a lot of the Supremes and the Temptations in this house.

"I guess there's no chance you can drive us back to the pool," I ask.

"Not unless a car drops out of the sky, brother."

I pour a giant glass of orange juice and chug it.

"Where's your show?" I ask.

"On the sidewalk."

"Nice place," I say. "Better not rain."

"Not supposed to."

"So, are you guys just setting up on a corner downtown, or what?"

Ki drums on the kitchen counter with his fingers. "No, it's a real gig. We got hired."

"For money?"

"Not money. Swag." He laughs. "Free hats!"

I laugh, too. "Good hats?"

"Like that," he says, pointing to my red baseball cap. "From Turn-It-Up."

"The music store?"

"Yeah. They're having a sidewalk sale. Asked us to provide live tunes. Bring the boys to watch."

"I will, but you'll be forcing us to support the enemy."

"How so?"

I tell him about the play-off schedule.

"I can be at Monday's game," he says. "Maybe Wednesday. I definitely have to work Tuesday night." Ki stocks shelves at a supermarket. He's saving up for college.

"What name is the band playing under tonight?" I ask. Ki and Tavo change the name every five minutes. "Agitavo? The Swarm?" Those are the most recent ones I can remember.

"Not sure yet." He rubs his chin.

"Maybe the Turnips."

He gives me a puzzled look.

"Long story," I say. "I'll tell you later."

I hear Griffin knocking on the door, so I run upstairs to change. "Tell him I'll be down in two seconds," I say. "Ask him who the Turnips are."

By the time we get to the pool we're dripping wet. Naturally, my parents are by the car, about to leave. So we'll have a nice hot walk back, too.

No problem. An hour submerged in that water will soothe anything.

My parents run over with a bottle of sunblock.

"I put that on before the game," I say.

"Take it," Mom insists. "Reapply it as soon as you get out of the water."

"Okay, Mom."

"And be sure to drink plenty," says my dad, handing me a water bottle.

"I know, Dad."

"And don't walk around barefoot on that hot cement."

"Right, Mom."

The boys are all laughing, but their parents would do the same thing.

"See you later," I say, hustling toward the entrance.

"Be sure to brush your teeth, Javon," Torry says with a smile.

"Don't pick your nose in public," Marcus adds.

They're all giggling. Big deal. My parents are great.

But really, don't baby me. Am I six years old?

Twice that.

THREE

Stepping Up

Griffin's parents have me over for a barbecue later. Then we walk up to Main Street for Ki's gig. Torry and Marcus said they'd meet us there.

"No dancing," Griffin says.

Earlier in the summer there was a dance at the pool, and I convinced him to go. I danced with a group of girls from school, but Griffin spent the whole time watching from the sidelines.

"You should try it," I say. "Nobody cares how bad you dance."

"I care," he says.

I can feel Ki's drumming over the sound of the band as we reach Main Street.

There are half a dozen people browsing through crates of used CDs under a canopy on the sidewalk. No one's really listening to the band. Ki and Tavo and the bass player are all wearing purple Turn-It-Up caps and the music is loud.

"I'm overheating," Griffin says. "Let's go inside."

I've never been in Turn-It-Up. We walk down the six cement steps to the entrance, which is below street level. The air conditioner is blasting. Ancient music from the Beatles is playing.

We poke around at the bins of records, which are mostly from the 1960s and 1970s. "Who buys this stuff?" I say. "Who even owns a record player?"

"You'd be surprised," says the guy at the counter. He has a blond ponytail and a tied-dyed T-shirt. "Vinyl is back."

I lift a Stevie Wonder album out of the bin and look at the names of the songs. I know a lot of them from Mom, but I've never seen a vinyl album up close before.

"We cool?" I say to Griffin. He nods and we go upstairs.

The crowd outside has doubled in size. I see Marcus and Torry approaching, too.

"We're going to take a quick break," Tavo says into the microphone. He pushes back his dreads, which don't fit so well under the purple cap. "Like three minutes. Stick around."

Ki's wearing a sleeveless green T-shirt that's soaked with sweat. He takes off his cap and wipes his short black hair with his palm. "You been practicing?" he asks me.

"Which? Baseball or drums?"

"Both. But you know that basic beat I showed you, right?"

"Sort of." Ki's only given me four drum lessons, and the furthest I've gone is a simple one-and-two-and-three-and-four pattern with the top cymbal and the snare. "Why?"

Ki starts to smile. "I might need you to sit in."

"You're joking, right?" I've barely had time to practice, with baseball and swimming and everything. We only have one drum kit, and Ki's always on it.

"I just want to sing one song, front and center," he says. "All we need is that basic beat in the background. Tavo and Ricky will provide the rhythm. You can handle it."

"Yeah, but . . ."

"One-and-two-and-three-and-four," he says, going through the motions in the air. Then he does it slower. "Let me see it."

I go through the same steps.

"Take a seat," Ki says. "Run through it for real."

Ki's drum stool is too high for me. "I'll stand for now," I say, pushing the stool aside.

Griffin is pointing at me, and Marcus and Torry are laughing. Nobody else in the crowd is paying attention, but that'll change when I start playing. Especially if I mess it up.

It was tricky at first to learn the pattern, but I'm good at hand-eye coordination so I nailed it pretty quickly. But I've never done this with anyone except Ki watching.

"What song?" I ask.

"You don't know it. I wrote it so it can work with that basic beat in the background. As I develop it, I'll make it more intricate."

"Can't you sing and play at the same time?"

"I can. I do. But I want to be the lead singer on this one. Out front for a change."

"Wow," I say, shaking my head. "Four lessons, and I'm already headlining at one of the biggest music festivals in Turn-It-Up history."

"Dreams do come true," Ki jokes. "Stay ready. I'll drum for two songs and then bring you up."

"Oh, man. I feel like I might bring something else up. Dinner."

"Jitters are part of the deal," he says. "Just tune out the crowd and play."

Yeah, like when I'm on the pitcher's mound. The difference is that I actually practice for that.

When I get back to my friends they're all like, "Let's go get some ice cream."

I shake my head. "I gotta stick around for Ki."

"It won't take long," Marcus says. He points up the street. "We'll just go to the Sweet Shop."

"Soon," I say. "A few minutes."

The band plays two songs with about a three-second break in between, and Tavo does some fast-paced rapping. Then Ki taps his sticks together and waves them at me.

"Be right back," I mumble to the boys.

Tavo steps aside and Ki moves to the microphone. He looks back at me and mouths, "One-and-two-and-three-and-four."

"When?" I whisper.

He points at me. "Now."

One-and-two-and-three-and-four. It's bad enough that I actually have to do this in front of an audience, but I've never even heard the song he's about to sing.

Just listen to your own beat, I think. It's like being a relief pitcher: a brief, intense burst.

I fall right into the pattern and it's almost automatic.

Ki's singing some soft words about the moonlight and someone's teasing smile. And then I see the reason he's doing this: Sherie Jackson. She's standing with some other girls, eyes on Ki.

He's mentioned her. She'll be a junior in high school this fall, a year behind Ki. She's a cashier at the same supermarket he works at.

One-and-two-and-three-and-four.

He finishes the song, looking down as he drags out the last "ni-i-i-i-ight."

People actually applaud this time. Sherie's laughing, but she's clapping, too.

Ki juts his thumb at me. "My brother," he says. People clap some more.

I hand him the sticks. Marcus and Torry have their arms folded, looking at me like they're in shock. Griffin gives me a light shove on the shoulder. "Awesome," he says.

"Let's get that ice cream," I say, starting to walk. I feel pretty good. Like I'm in a spotlight.

"Great job," Sherie says to me.

"Thanks."

"It's Javon, right?"

"Yeah." I point to my brother. "That's Ki."

Her friends crack up. Sherie looks slightly embarrassed. "Right," she says. "I know."

"He wrote that song," I tell her.

"I figured."

Her friends laugh again. Sherie rolls her eyes.

Ki starts pounding out a much more complicated rhythm. Tavo sings in a reggae style. His grandfather or somebody is from Jamaica, so he has a legitimate connection.

Marcus tilts up his thick glasses and looks at me like I have green hair or something. "I had no idea you could do that," he says. "Not bad at all."

"Ki's a good teacher. I still have to think about every action with the sticks, though. He says it'll be second nature for me after I've done it a billion times, like he has."

"He's great at it," Marcus says. "Makes me want to try."

"I'll show you that pattern sometime if you help me with that behind-the-back crossover dribble."

Marcus shakes his head. "That's a showboat move," he says. "I just fool around with it in the driveway."

"It looks good," I reply. "Putting on a show is all right. It can be effective." I'm thinking of Ki's move tonight. He could have stayed behind the drums and sung, but it's obvious he wanted to show off a little. I think it worked.

"A billion times, huh?" Marcus says. "How long would it take to dribble that many times, I wonder. A year, nonstop?"

Torry always seems to know the facts about things like that. He's really into science and math. "How many?" I ask him.

"There's more than 30 million seconds in a year," he says. "A billion would take at least 30 years, something in that range."

That's a lot of dribbling. I like my sports moments in shorter doses. Six strikes here, nine more there.

Can't wait for Monday.

"Time to turn Turn-It-Up into a turned-back team," I say.

"You're such a poet," Torry says. "Now what about that ice cream? I'm starving."

FOUR

Too Fast to See

Whatever the sport, play-offs always feel different. Each game takes on a huge importance. The bleachers are full for this one, and kids from the teams that finished back in the pack are lining the fences. Pennants are flapping in the breeze, and the field has been spruced up.

Griffin and I throw a ball back and forth in front of the dugout, not saying much. We'll be batting first, and the Turnips are out there for infield practice. Their starting pitcher looks sharp, whipping fastballs to the catcher.

The home plate umpire puts up his hand, then calls, "Batter up!"

I take a seat in the dugout, my home for at least three innings.

We get a nice jump. Griffin hits a double and Carlos drives him home with a deep single to right.

James pitches a solid game for us. By the time I get out to center field in the bottom of the fourth, we've built a 3–2 lead.

Lamar throws me a ball, and I toss it to Carlos in left. The sun is intense, so we're all wearing shades. Music is pumping from the announcer's booth between innings.

James strikes out the first two batters. He's a tall left-hander, with curly red hair sticking out from the back of his cap. His hair actually looks orange in contrast to the cap and the jersey.

The Turnips' pitcher steps into the batter's box and takes a few big cuts. He's probably the best player in the league, strong and fast. James clips the outside of the zone for a strike. The batter steps back, wipes his hands on his jersey, and gets back in his stance.

Pwock!

He clobbers the ball on a line drive, coming my way. I drift back, aware of the fence, and take a few quick steps to my left.

I've got it. A little jump, a little reach. Solidly in my glove for the third out.

I glance back. That ball would have cleared the fence. I saved a home run!

I lift up my glove and run in, holding it aloft.

Lots of cheers. Lamar smacks my back. James waits for me by the mound and slaps my hand.

The announcer says, "Nice play by number 6." He hesitates, probably looking for my name on the roster. Then he finds it. "Javon Park."

I draw a walk in my only time at bat, but Carlos pops out to leave me stranded on first. We still hold that razor-thin one-run lead going into the bottom of the sixth.

My time!

I'm good and ready, but I throw a half dozen warm-up pitches.

I take a quick glance around the field. Marcus and Torry are gripping the fence behind first base. My parents and Ki sit on the top row of the bleachers.

I kick at the dirt. My only blown saves of the entire season happened against this team. No more.

"Strike one!"

The batter hunkers down, twisting his hips and glowering. Griffin signals for a fastball.

"Strike two!"

Yes. I am already in the zone. Griffin calls for a curve, but I shake it off. Fastball. I nod.

"Strike three!"

Oh yeah. The noise gets louder. Griffin fires the ball to the third baseman, who throws to second, who flips it to the shortstop, who sends it to first. Around the horn.

The infielders start chattering. "No batter, Javon!" "More strikes."

The next guy isn't so easy to fool. He keeps fouling off my pitches, taking the occasional ball. The count goes full.

"Ball four!"

"No problem, Javon," Griffin calls as he throws me the ball.

"Turn two!" yells the shortstop. A double play will end this game.

But I'm still throwing strikes.

The batter takes a huge swing at my first pitch, missing by ten feet. I can just about taste those french fries—my postgame reward.

I unleash another fastball, and the batter's reaction stuns me. He taps a perfect bunt up the third baseline. I sprint in and scoop it up. But I don't even make the throw. When I look, the guy's already at first base.

I shake my head. No big deal.

"Any base!" Carlos yells from left field. With two base runners, there'd be force-outs at second or third. But I don't plan on letting anybody hit the ball.

"Strike one!"

"Mow 'em down, Javon!"

I glance at the on-deck batter. Their pitcher.

"Strike two!"

"One more time!"

Griffin pumps his fist at me. Punches his mitt.

"Strike three!"

Get out the ketchup.

Two outs. Two on.

A one-run lead. All eyes on me.

"Make him pay, Ernie," somebody yells from the Turnips' dugout.

The batter glares at me. He knows who stole that homer a couple of innings ago. I give him a mean smile. *Right, Ernie, that was me. Your worst nightmare.*

My first pitch is inside. Ernie doesn't even move his feet, he just leans back and watches it go by.

My second pitch is way off. It bounces in the dirt to the side of the plate and Griffin lunges for it. He leaps up and fakes a throw to first. The base runners scramble back.

Griffin calls time and trots to the mound.

"Settle down," he mumbles as he reaches me. "Throw strikes."

"No problem," I say. I know this guy can clear the bases in a second, so I don't want to feed him anything too easy. But I don't want to walk him either.

Lots more chatter. I focus on Griffin's glove. Fastball. A little low, but on target.

Ernie doesn't budge.

"Strike!"

Torry rattles the fence. I hear Ki yelling, "Two more!"

Yeah. Just like that. Too fast to see.

I feel a surge of energy. Grip that ball. Rear back and fire.

Smack!

The ball takes flight, same path as before, rising just slightly as it zooms toward center.

Be there, James!

Not this time.

The Turnips rush from the dugout as the ball lands with a crash deep in the parking lot. I stand there with my mouth hanging open as the first runner scores, then the second. Ernie rounds third with his arms in the air, then leaps and lands with both feet on the plate. They mob him.

Disaster.

I don't even move. Lamar trots over and squeezes my shoulder. Griffin pulls me toward the dugout.

Coach just says, "Tough loss. We'll even the series tomorrow."

My teammates all tell me to shake it off. "You pitched good." "We'll bounce right back."

But I know I blew it.

Long night ahead.

I couldn't eat a french fry if I tried.

FIVE

Taking Chances

Ki throws his arm across my shoulder. "It happens to everybody," he says. "You put yourself out there like that and sometimes you get burned."

I blink hard. My parents tell me I did great. Torry and Marcus say the same thing.

I turn back to the field. The Turnips are huddled around their coach, looking all excited. The kid who hit the game-winning homer, Ernie, has his cap on backward and is grinning wide. That was supposed to be us.

"Do you want to ride home with us?" Dad asks.

I just shake my head and look down.

"We'll cheer him up," Torry tells my father.

"He'll snap out of it with an ice cream cone," Marcus adds.

Ki says he'll walk home with us, too. Within three blocks, the other guys are way ahead, joking around. Griffin seems to be taking the loss in stride. But he isn't the one who gave up that home run.

So it's just me and Ki.

"Like I was saying," Ki says, "about taking a chance and putting yourself out there. You can't ever win if you're afraid of losing."

I say "yeah," but it comes out so soft I don't think he hears me.

"You get knocked down, you stand back up. That's how it is in sports."

I nod. He puts his hand on top of my head. I'm not quite five feet tall, so he has a good ten inches on me.

"Remember Saturday night?" he says. "I mean, talk about taking a chance. I got out there and sang that song . . . . I sang my heart out."

"It was awesome."

"Right. So I look around after we finish the set, but she's gone."

"Sherie?"

"Yeah, who else? I sang my guts out, man. I wrote that song about her."

"She noticed," I say.

He lets out a short, huffy laugh. "Yeah, she noticed. And she took off."

We walk a few more blocks in silence.

"What made you write that song?" I ask.

"I don't know." He shakes his head. "One night after work, we were both punching out at the same time. I stood with her in the parking lot while she waited for her parents to pick her up. I made some jokes about stocking shelves—how I lifted three tons of weights that night, one sixteen-ounce can of beans at a time. She laughed. That's about it."

"She came to the gig."

He shrugs.

The guys are waiting at the next corner.

"Summertime!" Torry calls. "Ice cream time." He points toward the Sweet Shop.

I guess I'm getting a little hungry.

"Listen," Ki says, "we can mope for five more minutes. Then we start looking ahead. You've got another shot at that team tomorrow night."

"Right. Thanks." I can feel my confidence easing back.

The Sweet Shop is packed. I read all twenty-eight flavors while we're waiting. Blueberry almond sounds good.

"So what about you?" I whisper to Ki. "Think you'll get a second chance?"

"I never had a first one," he says. "But I got a good song out of it." He smiles. "Still a lot of summer left. Who knows?"

The five years between Ki and me has always seemed like a huge gap. Ki treats me like I'm his favorite person in the whole world, and I look up to him for everything. But I don't ever remember seeing him have a setback. Probably because I never paid attention to that, or he never bothered me with his troubles.

"You have money?" I ask him. I don't.

"Sure. Get a double scoop."

We sit on a bench in front of the shop, just watching cars go by. Marcus asks Ki to teach him some drum moves.

"It'd help if I had a drum," Ki says with a laugh. He taps a rhythm on the bench: one-two-three-bop, one-two-three-bop. "Come to the house later. I'll show you."

I finish the blueberry almond and start in on the bottom scoop, cherry vanilla. Torry says it's too bad I couldn't pitch and play center field at the same time. "I mean, you robbed Ernie of that first homer. If James could jump a little, he would have done the same thing."

"A little? That ball was ten feet over his head. The one I got would have barely cleared the fence."

"Still," Torry says.

"Still what? It was a good pitch. He found it. Sent it into no-man's-land."

"I guess."

"No excuses," I say. "But man, those guys have my number. Three games, three blown saves."

They all come to our house and we go down to the basement. My dad put up a wall to split the basement in half a few years ago, and this side has a pool table, the drum set, a freezer, and a bin for our sports equipment. The furnace is on the other side of the wall with tools and storage boxes.

Ki shows them that four-beat thing. "This is what Javon was playing the other night," he says, drumming gently as he talks. "An easy pattern. You master that, and then you add a step. A little at a time."

He picks up a big drum from the floor, like a single bongo. "This is from West Africa," he says. "Good drum to learn on. Watch."

He taps the edge of the drum. "Right, left, right, then center. Fingertips on the edges, then flat hand in the middle of the drum. Right, left, right, center."

"Amazing how much music you get from that," Marcus says.

"It's way more than music," Ki says. "It's uplifting. It's healing."

Ki hands him the drum. Marcus taps it slowly, speaking out loud. "Right, left, right, center. Cool!"

Now I understand why Ki plays his drums in the middle of the night sometimes. I hear him in the basement while I'm lying in bed. It's like what I do when I'm frustrated or angry. I'll throw a ball at a pitch-back for hours at a time, or shoot baskets in the driveway. It's better than staring at the ceiling.

"Tavo and me, we get five or six guys together and just drum like that," Ki says. "Much faster, of course. You can go for hours, changing the rhythm anytime you want. Like I said, you master one pattern and add on."

"One step at a time," Marcus says. "Sounds familiar. I think maybe my dad tells me that. Like every other minute!"

"Here we go," Ki says. He hands Griffin and Torry small drums, too. Turns over a plastic trash can and tells me to use that. Then he starts in, and we all join. In a few minutes, we actually have a rhythm going.

I feel it all the way through me. Before, my drumming was just a matter of repeating a pattern. It's still that, but I get what Ki's saying now. About it lifting you up.

I might do some drumming before tomorrow night's game. Seems like a great way to get ready for anything.

SIX

Reflex Actions

My confidence lasted about two seconds. As soon as I got into bed I started worrying. I pitch well against everybody except Turn-It-Up, and in less than twenty-four hours I might be facing them again. Maybe Coach will make the smart move and not use me as the closer.

Against the Turnips, I might as well be called "the opener." I open the door and they run through it to victory.

Go to sleep, I tell myself. Like that would work. The only way to fall asleep is to not think about it. Think about something else.

Not baseball either.

One-and-two-and-three-and four.

Ball one, ball two, ball three. Walk.

Strike one, strike two, foul ball. Homer.

Oh, man. This could be a long night.

So I play a drum solo in my mind. Simple. Slow. Yawn.

I wake up to a bright morning and the smell of omelets. Dad's taking a day off from work, so he's cooking. Mom's due at the hospital in half an hour. She's a nurse practitioner.

Dad points at me as I step into the kitchen. "This one's yours," he says. "No cheese."

I eat just about anything, but cheese tastes bad to me. "So what do I have in there?"

"Red peppers, onion, chickpeas, and salsa."

Mom is sipping coffee. "Did you hear your brother moving at all?" she asks.

"Not a peep," I say.

"No surprise," she says. "He was still drumming after midnight when I fell asleep."

"Really? I never heard him." I guess I nodded off quicker than I thought.

Dad sets a plate in front of me. I grind some pepper on the omelet. "Looks good. Do they make omelets like this in Korea?"

"Even better," he says. "Similar to that, but you roll it up in a sheet of dried seaweed."

I wince. "Oh." He had me try seaweed once. It's better than cheese, but not much. Sort of fishy.

"It's an acquired taste," he says. "Give it another try sometime."

"Maybe next year."

"Same for you, Lauryn?" he asks Mom.

"Sounds good," she says. "Extra salsa. And you can hold the seaweed."

Dad laughs. "We don't even have any. I've become too American!"

"Oh yeah," I say. "You're a regular Yankee-Doodle."

He starts whistling the song.

"I might be late for the game," Mom says. "I'll be working until at least six."

"No problem," I say. "You know I never play the first three innings."

"Make sure you eat."

I nod. "I'm eating now."

"Dinner. A real dinner. Last time I worked late, you ate potato chips and three ice-cream sandwiches."

"They were very filling."

"I'm sure they were."

"I'll eat some seaweed to round it out."

"Very funny." She finishes her last bite of eggs and dabs at her mouth. "Excellent breakfast, Nam."

My father and my brother have the same name: Ki-Nam Park. But they use different parts of it. Obviously.

Ki comes clomping down the stairs.

"Late night," Mom says. "Writing another song?"

"Not exactly." Ki looks all serious this morning. Hope he's not too down about that girl thing. "I was just playing around," he says. "It helps me think."

I catch Ki's eye and tap out that four-beat rhythm on the table. He taps the same in response.

"Upbeat?" I say.

"Getting there."

Griffin calls me in the middle of the afternoon. He says Torry and Marcus went to the pool and were hoping we'd follow. But I just want to chill out at home today. I tell Griffin I'll meet him at five o'clock to walk to the field.

Ki's at work, so the drums are free.

Slow at first.

One-and-two-and-three-and-four.

Faster.

One-and-two-and-three-and-four, cymbal.

Within a minute I'm not even counting it out. It's becoming a reflex, almost like breathing. Time for Ki to show me the next step.

One thing he does is put on some music and play along with it. I check the CDs on the shelf and insert one he listens to all the time. I try to hold my pattern but keep it at the same pace as the songs.

It's amazing how fast two hours can go.

I hustle upstairs and make a peanut butter sandwich. Griffin will be here any minute. Where's my glove? Where's my cap?

Breathe, Javon. You just got rid of all that tension. Don't bring it back at game time.

I suit up and wolf down the sandwich. Head back to the cellar for one last round of drumming.

Let out my breath. Pick up the sticks. Fall into that rhythm.

Ready for anything.

SEVEN

Fine Lines

Carlos is pitching for us tonight, and he's sharper than ever through the first two innings. We build a 4–0 lead on James's double and Griffin's home run, and things are looking good for a deciding game tomorrow.

The dilemma is, who'll pitch that game? James threw five innings last night and Carlos is pitching now, so our two regular starters won't be eligible. Lamar is the most likely choice.

Or me. But I've never pitched longer than an inning all season. And we have to finish this one before thinking about tomorrow.

"Let's go, Lamar!" I call, shaking the fence in front of the dugout. I want a big lead when I take the mound. No more of these one-run nail-biters.

But Lamar strikes out. Inning over.

Coach sends me to center field in the top of the fourth. (We're the home team today.) I see my mom parking her car out past the right-field foul pole. She's still in her green scrubs, so she must have come straight from work. My father's been here the whole game.

Carlos has not allowed a single base runner yet. Perfect game.

I left my sunglasses in the dugout, so I'm squinting in the sun. The days keep getting hotter. We could use a good storm to cool things off.

First batter hits a fly ball my way. Nice and high, easy to get under. I make the catch and throw the ball in.

Carlos yields a walk and James bobbles an easy grounder at shortstop for an error. But we get out of the inning with no harm, except to the perfect game. Carlos settles down and gets three straight outs in the fifth.

In the bottom of the inning, Coach taps me on the shoulder. I'll be batting third.

"How's your arm?" Coach asks.

"Fine," I say. "Looks like Carlos can cruise through the whole game though."

"Be ready just in case," he says. "His pitches are losing their zip."

I step to the on-deck circle. I'm not there for long. Griffin sends a lazy grounder to the first baseman, who grabs it and steps on the bag. Two out already.

Griffin gives me a sheepish smile as he trots past me. "I tried to hammer it," he says. "Barely nicked it, though."

The guy pitching for the Turnips has an awkward motion, almost sidearm. It's distracting. I watch a strike go by, right down the middle. A great pitch to hit, but I realize it too late.

The infielders yell, "No batter!" just like every infield in the history of baseball. Try harder, guys.

The second pitch is way outside, and I take it for a ball.

"Good eye!" call my teammates. We're not very original either.

The third pitch is high. The next one is higher.

I watch ball four go by and roll my bat toward the dugout.

Home Run Ernie's playing first base tonight. He nods as I reach the base but doesn't have any expression. I nod back.

Torry and Marcus are by the fence. I raise my fist at them. They yell, "Go, Javon!"

I take a short lead. I'm fast. I can score from here on a double. Maybe even on a deep single if I get a jump. There are two outs, so I can run on the pitch.

Zoom. I'm sprinting toward second as soon as the ball is released.

"Slide!" yells Griffin. I outrun the throw by half a beat.

"Safe!"

When Carlos drills the next pitch up the middle, I score with ease. It's 5–0 now. A nice cushion.

Coach is right about Carlos's pitch speed. He gets one out in the sixth, then gives up a double and a walk.

Coach calls time-out and strides toward the mound. He talks to Carlos and Griffin, then waves me in.

Don't panic, I think. But I'm starting to. Coach hands me the ball.

Griffin raises his fist and pushes it toward me, putting pressure on my shoulder.

In the spotlight again. I swallow hard. The announcer says, "Taking the mound for Pedraza's: number 6, Javon Park."

I throw a few warm-up pitches, then signal to the umpire that I'm ready.

But am I? My arm's a little stiff, and my control is off. I walk the first batter on four pitches.

Bases loaded. Don't let this happen again!

I do a quick evaluation in my head. Gotta get these next two outs or Ernie will be up. That's all I need. Waste this lead and it'll haunt me all summer.

I throw another ball. Five in a row.

I finally throw a good pitch, but the batter lines it between first and second for a single. Lamar gets it in here fast, but a run scores.

I shut my eyes and let out my breath.

Coach calls time. Again. Walks toward the mound. Is he yanking me already?

"You okay, Javon?"

"I think so."

"Settle down. Let's get an out."

"Or two," Griffin adds. He stares right at me. "No batter."

I look over at Ernie, swinging two bats in the on-deck circle. Bases loaded, 5–1, only one out. Do the math. This could be trouble.

"Strike one!"

"Atta boy!" Griffin yells and throws the ball back.

"Any base!" calls Carlos.

The next pitch is slightly outside, but I think it's in the zone. The umpire calls it a ball.

I twist my shoulders to loosen up. Grip that ball hard. Take Griffin's signal and focus.

The ball's hit sharply, bouncing up the middle. James scoops it up, steps on second, and fires the ball to first.

Double play! Game over. Finally! I drop to my knees and look at the sky.

Griffin runs out and whacks me on the arm. James pulls my cap down over my eyes, and everybody else acts like I just won the World Series.

That's just relief. I didn't pitch well at all. But now we've set up a one-game championship, and we're the team with momentum.

"You saved that one," I say to James. "Not me."

"Team effort," he says. "That's baseball."

We shake hands with the Turnips. "See you tomorrow," I say to Ernie.

"Man, I wanted that last at bat," he says. "We were rallying."

"That was an illusion," says Griffin, who's behind me in line.

"We'll find out tomorrow," Ernie replies. "May the best team win."

"Count on it," Griffin says.

Big difference after this game. Last night we had our heads down and barely said a word, while the Turnips celebrated and laughed. Tonight we're all lively and confident. The Turnips look deflated.

Which will it be tomorrow night? Triumph or defeat?

EIGHT

Driveway Hoops

Torry insists that we play some basketball Wednesday morning. "It'll take your mind off the game," he says on the phone.

"It'll tire us out!"

"When are you ever tired? One game," he says.

"I will if Griffin will."

"I already called him. He's on his way over."

"Okay. But not you and Marcus against us." They always trounce us when we go two-on-two.

"You and me," Torry says. "My house."

I peel an orange and look for my basketball sneakers, which I haven't worn in a while.

I'm stunned when I step outside. It's only eight thirty and already hot. We'll have to hit the pool later or we'll never make it through the afternoon.

Torry and Marcus live across the street from each other, a block and a half from my house. I'm there in minutes. The three of them are shooting baskets in Torry's driveway, which is narrow but has a key and a free-throw line.

"Nice job getting out of that jam last night," Marcus says, bouncing a ball to me.

"Thanks." I take a shot and it bonks off the rim. "Of course, I created the jam. Haven't exactly been sharp this week."

"Maybe tonight," Torry says. "Something tells me it'll go down to the wire."

"Always does with the Turnips," I say.

I cover Marcus just to mix things up, since he and Torry go one-on-one every day. Marcus is taller than me and has better skills. But Torry is way better than Griffin, so we build a quick lead.

Marcus hits a couple of lay-ups to make it close. His reach is just a little too much for me.

Torry's dad comes out with a pitcher of iced tea.

"Stay hydrated, boys," he says.

"All right," Torry says as the ball rolls into the yard after I miss a shot. "Break."

"Thanks, Mr. S.," I say as he hands me a glass.

Torry gets the ball and tosses it to his dad. He sinks a long jumper, even in dress shoes and a tie.

"Heading to work?" I ask before realizing how obvious that is.

"Mm-hmm. See you at lunch, Torry?"

"Yeah." The accounting office is right up on Main Street, so Marcus and Torry can drop in on their dads anytime. My father works across town at city hall.

"What's the score?" I ask.

"Who knows?" Griffin replies. "You win."

"It's 15–11," Torry says. "We gotta finish. Just to 21."

"Why do we have to finish?" Griffin asks. "I just presented you with the victory. Accept it graciously."

"We have to finish
because we started,"
Torry says definitively. "It's
a matter of principle."

"Let's vote," Griffin says.

Torry laughs. "No voting."

Griffin gulps down the rest of
his iced tea. "I vote that you win."
He thinks this is funny.

Marcus votes to keep playing.

I know Torry. He really does think it matters. Not who wins or loses, but that we finish the game. So I vote to keep playing.

"Our ball," I say.

Torry steps back and hits a three-pointer.

Marcus makes a lay-up.

"You gotta try," Torry says to Griffin.

"I am trying."

Torry lunges forward like he's going to drive, then passes me the ball and drifts back. I pass. He nails another three. Game over.

"Was that so hard?" Torry asks.

"Not for you," Griffin says.

73

He flops onto the side steps and wipes his face with the front of his shirt. "It'll be brutal tonight."

"Tough it out," Marcus says. "All or nothing. Champs or chumps."

Griffin is a little less competitive than the rest of us. But once he's in the heat of the action, he doesn't let up. At least not in a real game. Driveway basketball isn't quite the same.

Torry's different. He could play two-on-two basketball all day long, and every game would be just as intense as any other.

I'm that way, too. Maybe I'm only 98 percent as intense as Torry, but that's a lot.

"Anybody ready for another one?" Torry asks.

Okay, maybe 97 percent. "I'm done," I say. "I do have a baseball game later, remember?"

Torry picks up the ball and starts shooting free throws. The rest of us sit in the shade and watch. He keeps count and hits 72 out of 100.

"That your best?" Griffin asks.

Torry shakes his head. "Seventy-four. I need to get to 80 by the end of the summer."

"Why?"

"Just because."

My bet is he'll do it by the end of the week. Numbers and percentages are important to him. Maybe because his father's an accountant.

"Time to swim?" Torry asks.

"Yeah." I'm not looking forward to the walk, but that water will feel great. "No racing."

Torry nods.

"No tag, either. Just relaxing. Game prep."

"Ping-Pong?" Torry says. "Shuffleboard?"

"Swimming," I say. "Or floating. That's all."

Torry shakes his head. "Marcus will play Ping-Pong, right?"

"Sure," Marcus says.

"Tomorrow, though," Torry tells me. "Baseball's over. Basketball, shuffleboard, everything. No more excuses. Be ready."

NINE

Unplayable

Even Torry admitted it was uncomfortably hot this afternoon, so we played video games in Griffin's air-conditioned house after the pool. I left at three thirty and flopped on my bed for an hour.

"Is there such a thing as it being too hot to play?" Griffin asks as we reach Main Street.

We've only walked halfway to the field but it looks like we swam here. I wipe my face with my glove, which isn't the least bit absorbent. So I wipe it with my cap, which isn't much better.

"It's gotta be a hundred," Griffin says.

"Ninety-two," I reply. "It's the humidity that makes it bad."

Griffin takes a drink from his water bottle. "I'm going to melt under all my gear."

The edge of the sky looks like a bruise—purple and hazy.

Ernie and a couple of other Turnips are tossing a ball around on the diamond when we reach the field. Lamar is the only one of our teammates there. He's sitting in the dugout by himself.

"You pitching?" Griffin asks him.

"Looks like it. Coach told me to be ready."

"Did he tell you to be early?" I ask.

Lamar shrugs. "I've been here an hour. Figured I might be less nervous at the field."

"Did it work?"

"Nah."

Coach enters the dugout and tells Lamar to warm up real slow. Then he looks at me. "You may be going longer than an inning tonight," he says. "You're our only relief option, so be ready."

"Who's pitching for Turn-It-Up?" I ask.

"I don't know. We've faced their best pitchers, so their situation is the same as ours. Nobody's

77

allowed to pitch with only one day of rest if they've gone more than three innings."

Griffin and Lamar walk away to warm up.

A big breeze sweeps across the field, but it's hot air. No relief. That bruise looks bigger, covering more sky. Time to start.

The Turnips' pitcher played shortstop for the first two games of the series. He's fast, but wild. Our first two batters go down swinging.

"Come on, Griffin!" I call. "Get it started."

But he strikes out, too.

I help Griffin strap on the chest protector.

"Bad start," Griffin says. "Long way to go."

I look around and see my parents squeezing into the bleachers, but not Ki. He's working.

Lamar's a deceptive pitcher, short but powerful. He walks a batter and gives up a single, but we get out of the inning. No harm.

The sky is quite dark now, and the wind is whipping around. I haven't heard any thunder.

Carlos steps up to bat. He lines the first pitch into right field for a single. We all stand up and holler. "Here we go!" I say.

I feel a few drops. No big deal. People raise umbrellas in the bleachers.

The pitcher throws one over the catcher's head, and Carlos streaks toward second. He doesn't even have to slide.

We start yelling for James to drive him home. The drops get bigger and steadier.

And then it's a cloudburst.

Whoa! It's like buckets coming down. The umpire raises both arms. "Rain delay!" he calls. All of the players run to the dugouts. The parents run to their cars.

Both coaches go out to talk with the umpire. When ours comes back he says to stay in the dugout. "As long as there's no lightning, we might get the game in," he says. "It might pass in a hurry."

Or it might not.

Twenty minutes later, the rain is still pouring and the base paths are turning to slop.

"Not looking good," Coach says. "How's your arm, James?"

"Feels all right."

"You're allowed to pitch tomorrow, but I don't want you to overdo it," Coach says. "Assuming you're okay, we'll start Lamar for an inning or two, then bring you in."

There's an inch of water in the dugout, so I pull my feet up on the bench. "Guess that means Ernie will be on the mound for them," I say.

Coach looks across the field. "Most likely."

The umpire comes over, holding an umbrella. "It's unplayable," he says. "Weather report says this'll be over soon, but the field's a mess."

So we're done.

The storm ends as quickly as it began.

I meet my parents outside the fence. "Well, that was a bust," I say.

"At least Ki can be here tomorrow," Mom says. "He didn't want to miss this."

I step around a huge puddle. The sun is out, and it doesn't feel much cooler.

"What did you eat for supper?" Mom asks. She worked late again.

"Another peanut butter sandwich. And a banana." I put on my sunglasses. "And you?"

"Ha! Today was crazy. I haven't eaten since lunchtime, and that was coffee and a yogurt."

"We're going for pizza," Dad says. "Want to come?"

"Can I walk home? Maybe Griffin and me will get some ice cream."

"Don't be out late," Dad says, handing me cash.

No sign of Torry or Marcus tonight. Guess they heard the storm was coming.

"We would've won that game," Griffin says as we reach Main Street. "But tomorrow's a different story. Ernie's a big-game pitcher. That'll be tough."

82

Three of the Turnips are waiting in line at the Sweet Shop. I give them a thumbs-up.

"I'm getting the exact opposite of what I had the other night," I say. "Blueberry almond on the bottom, and cherry vanilla on top."

"Very radical," Griffin says. "Just to prove how different I am from you, I'm going very traditional. Two scoops of chocolate."

"Impressive."

"Are we eating inside or out?" he asks.

"Inside," I say. "Wet benches, and still too hot."

We take a seat at a booth. I'm focusing on my top scoop when Griffin nudges me. "Ki's here."

And he's not alone. Ki doesn't see us, so I watch as he and Sherie study the flavors. She laughs at something he says. He does a little dance move with his shoulders.

They get cones and Ki pays. He sees me and blushes. They walk over and he slides in next to Griffin. Sherie sits next to me.

"Hi, Javon," she says.

"Hi." I look at Ki. He lifts one side of his mouth in a dumb grin.

"We got rained out," I say.

"We figured." Ki wraps a napkin around his cone and hands one to Sherie.

She's smiling at me.

"I heard the storm," Ki replies. "It was over before we got out of work though."

Sherie giggles. Why, I don't know.

"So, Ki," I say, glancing sideways at Sherie. "You read anything good lately? Or written anything?"

He kicks my leg under the table and rubs his fist with his other hand. "Not today," he says.

"Maybe later, huh? In the moonlight."

Sherie laughs again. "You two are funny."

Ki asks about the game. There's not much to tell. "I sat for a scoreless inning. Then I sat through the rain delay. We'll try again at six o'clock tomorrow. Can you be there?"

"Day off," he says. "I'll be there."

Griffin asks Sherie if she likes baseball.

"Sure. I played softball when I was your age."

"No more?" I ask.

"She runs track," Ki says. "She'd beat any of us by a mile in a sprint. We could be a relay team and she'd still beat us by herself."

Sherie shrugs. "I work hard at it."

I finish my ice cream. Griffin's holding his up and letting it drip into his mouth from a hole in the bottom of the cone.

"We'd better go," I say.

Sherie gets up to let me out. "Good luck tomorrow," she says.

"Thanks. We need it."

"Tell Mom I'll be home in like an hour," Ki says. He holds out his fist and I bump it.

I'm pretty lucky already. I've got the best brother in the world. So I don't need to be lucky tomorrow, just tough.

TEN

Next Step

I seem to be staying awake longer every night, but it's summer. I let my mind go wherever it wants for a change, and I keep seeing Ernie at the plate, ready to wallop one of my pitches over the fence.

My fists are clenched. Gotta relax. So I shift that image a bit. I see Ernie swinging fiercely at my pitches and missing, the ball popping into Griffin's glove and the umpire yelling "Strike!"

That's more like it.

I run the bases in my head, hands up after smacking a game-winning home run. The farthest ball I've ever hit didn't get within twenty feet of the fence, of course, but maybe that day will come.

My window's open because there's finally a cool breeze. I stop thinking about baseball. Think about floating in the pool. Or sitting in the yard with a grilled hamburger and a cold iced tea.

Crickets are chirping and a plane rumbles overhead. Nice sounds. They make it easier to sleep . . .

I wake up and close my blinds because the full moon is shining on my bed. I slept three hours and need a lot more than that, but I hear Ki drumming in the basement, so I go down.

He looks up and smiles.

"I don't know if it's good or bad to hear you playing the drums at two o'clock in the morning," I say.

"Drumming's always good," he says. "Even when you feel bad." He rattles out a quick rhythm: cymbals, bass, snare.

"You feel good tonight?"

"Extra good."

I pick up the single bongo and pat it a few times. "What happened?"

He taps the snare. "I was on my break tonight, drinking some juice behind the store. She comes out on her break, too. We're like 'hot day' and 'might rain,' you know? Nothing much. She goes, 'Nice night for ice cream,' and I'm like, 'Yeah.' And I'm wondering if that's just a statement or a hint, so I go, 'I'll buy you one. You done at seven?'"

He runs through that beat again, faster. I try to keep up on the bongo.

"Did she mention your song?" I ask.

"Nah. And thanks a lot, bro. Like I needed you pointing that out."

"I didn't. Not directly." We both laugh.

I look around the cellar. My old tricycle is in the corner, and the skateboard I haven't touched all summer. There's a box full of toys from when I was little.

We should probably have a yard sale.

"How long have you been down here?" I ask.

"Since about ten."

He taps out a new beat and I try to follow on the bongo. Doesn't take long for me to get it. We go softly for a half hour until I start yawning.

"You should get to bed," Ki says. "I'm off tomorrow, but you've got that game."

"I'm okay," I say. "I'd rather drum."

"Switch places," he says, standing up. "You're ready for the next lesson."

He lowers the height of the stool for me. "Two beats on the tom, four on the snare," he says. "So it's like BOP-bop, BOP-bop, bah-bah-bah-bah, BOP-bop, BOP-bop . . ."

"Okay." I run through and mess up about every other beat.

He mimics it on the bongo.

I do better the second time. Still better the third.

I keep going and Ki joins in. He's sitting on the

floor with two drums between his knees, just improvising. Sounds good. Feels good.

I concentrate on the pattern. It'll take a few days for it to stick, but for now I'm just enjoying this. Mistakes don't mean a thing when you're jamming.

I'm starting to sweat and getting thirsty. "Enough?" I ask him.

"Enough."

Mom and Dad brought home their leftover pizza, so we warm up two slices and pour some orange juice.

"Tired?" he asks.

"Relaxed. But yeah, I'll sleep." The game seems far away now. Less of a worry.

"That zone is so cool, when I'm drumming," Ki says. "And it works if you're alone or drumming with a group. When I'm by myself it's soothing and you can get really deep into your thoughts."

I started feeling that tonight.

"It's all good," he says, taking a last bite of pizza. "Even if I don't have a drum, I can imagine that I do, and it settles me down. Or helps break the monotony when I'm stocking shelves." He breaks into a big grin. "One can, two cans, three cans, four!" He pats it out on the table.

I yawn and shut my eyes.

"Up, brother," he says. "Get to bed."

"Yeah. You?"

"Yeah. Good day . . . good day. I didn't want it to end."

"It ended three hours ago!" I say.

He nods. "This is a good one, too. Let's do it again soon. No limits."

I start up the stairs.

"Tomorrow," Ki says. "Big game. Biggest of your life so far. Enjoy it, Javon. Win, lose, whatever happens. Enjoy it. Like drumming. It's all good."

ELEVEN

We Need a Rally

My pregame routine is pretty standard. A sandwich an hour and a half before, a walk to the field with Griffin, some warm-up throws, batting practice. No need to alter that today. So what if the entire season is on the line?

The outfield is mushy in spots from last night's rain, but the base paths have been rolled and are in good shape.

Lamar and James are both throwing pitches, but Coach says Lamar will start. The crowd is gathering. Torry and Marcus walk by with a sign that says **GO PEDRAZA'S!** in red marker.

"Nice!" I call. "Very clever, too. How did you ever think of that?"

Marcus grins. "It was Torry's idea."

Torry bows. "You better win," he says. "I put a lot of work into this. At least a minute."

I notice a familiar drumbeat from the bleachers. Ki and Tavo are up in the top row, pounding African drums. Sherie is there, too.

It's like the whole season has been funneled into this one game.

"Make it good," Torry says. "See you after."

Lamar gets in a jam almost immediately. In the bottom of the first, the Turnips' leadoff batter doubles and Lamar issues a walk. We get an out on a pop-up behind the plate. Then Ernie whacks one deep off the left-field fence to bring in two runs.

Griffin walks to the mound. I can't hear him, but I know what he says when a pitcher's in trouble. He's done it for me a thousand times. Settle. Concentrate on the batter. One pitch at a time.

Griffin doesn't panic, and he's a big reason we're playing for the title.

Lamar strikes out the next two batters. I hold out my palm and he slaps it, but he looks shaken.

"Get 'em right back!" Griffin says. But Ernie is throwing hard for the Turnips, and nobody's making contact. Three up, three down for us in the top of the second.

Surprisingly, Coach sends Lamar back to the mound. James is ready to go, and he's a better pitcher.

The strategy doesn't work. Lamar's first pitch is lined into center for a single. His second is way outside and Griffin can't reach it. Man on second. No outs.

Another single makes it 3–0. Lamar kicks at the mound. Coach calls time-out. He sends Lamar out to right field and Carlos takes over at shortstop so James can pitch.

James gets us out of the inning. We're in a hole, but not too bad. I clap as my teammates run to the dugout.

Lamar slumps in the corner of the dugout and pulls his cap down. I slide over.

"Don't sweat it," I say.

He sniffs and wipes his eyes. "I got clobbered."

"We all do sometimes. We'll bounce back."

But we don't. Nobody's hitting Ernie today. Three ups and we've still got a big zero on the board.

"You'll pinch hit to lead off the fourth," Coach tells me as James cruises through the bottom of the third. "Then go out to center."

"Think I'll pitch later?"

"Maybe. If we can get a lead," he says. "James looks good, though. We'll see what develops."

It would be fine with me if James pitches the rest of the way. I haven't been my best this week.

I pull on a batting glove and swing a few times. I've been studying Ernie's pitches. His control is good, and he's hitting a certain spot. A little low, a little outside. Hittable, but fast.

96

There's more noise when I stride to the plate. Torry wiggles the sign he made. The drums echo briefly. The catcher smacks his glove and grunts.

First pitch is right where I expected. I watch it go by, and the umpire calls a strike.

The Turnips yell this time. "Two more, Ernie!" "He can't hit!"

Second pitch is in the dirt. I know what's coming next.

Yep, same spot as before. I make great contact. The ball scoots through the hole between first and second. First hit we've had all game.

More bongos. Lots of yelling from our bench.

Ernie looks a little rattled. Carlos sends a soaring double deep into right, and I sprint around the bases. Coach waves me in, and I slide for a run as the ball gets cut off at second.

I hop right up and brush the dirt from my pants. Slap hands with everybody. Lamar pumps both fists, left, right. We're back in this thing.

But the inning ends quickly. It's 3–1, Turnips.

I grab my shades and trot to center field, sidestepping a puddle behind second base.

Ernie is on fire today, both hitting and pitching. He rips one down the left-field line and it bounces all the way to the fence for another double. But

James gets a pair of strikeouts. The inning ends safely as I run in and grab a fly ball behind second.

Two more innings. Two runs behind. We need a rally. James hits a leadoff single and another guy walks. Two on, one out, and I'm up. Maybe this is my day to be a batting hero.

Maybe not. I hit a weak foul ball that dribbles behind first base. I watch a called strike that I thought was outside. My last swing finds air.

Carlos whiffs, too. We're running out of innings.

Lamar and I trot side by side to the outfield.

"Think we have a chance?" he asks.

"Always a chance," I say. "We're in it until the final out."

James strikes out the side.

"That was easy," Lamar says as we trot back.

"Start the rally," I say. He'll be leading off.

Lamar hasn't done much with the bat this series. He's struck out twice already today. But he lays down a nice bunt and beats the throw to first.

We all stand. Griffin's at bat. Our power hitter. If ever there was a time for a home run, this is it.

"Strike one!"

"Find your pitch!" I call.

Griffin taps the plate with his bat. Glares at Ernie.

"Strike two!"

Griffin yanks on his sleeve, then adjusts the brim of his helmet. Ernie shakes off a sign, then goes into his windup.

Whack! The ball rises and soars, deep into right. The outfielders just turn and watch it go. I lift both arms. Home run!

We're tied. Whole new ball game.

We run out to the plate. Lamar scores first, pumping his fist. Griffin sprints from third to home, but he doesn't celebrate.

I pat his back. "Let's get one more," he says.

But the next three guys strike out.

Bottom of the sixth. If they score, it's over.

Coach points to center field. Fine with me.

A breeze picks up, and a flag sways above the announcer's booth. No clouds tonight.

Ping. A single up the middle. A small splash pops up when it crosses the puddle, but I field the ball easily and toss it in.

The next batter runs the count full, then James slips a third strike past him. Their shortstop fouls off a bunch of pitches, then he strikes out, too.

But James has thrown a lot of pitches. He walks the next two batters to load the bases, and suddenly it looks like he couldn't find the plate with a searchlight.

Coach calls time. He waves both arms toward me. Bases loaded. Guess who's up?

I swallow hard and walk to the mound. James hands me the ball. "My arm's spent," he says. "Finish this thing."

He runs out to center.

Ernie's in the batter's box. Griffin turns and tells him to back off. "He needs to warm up!"

I feel like I could puke right here on the mound. I take a breath. Ki and Tavo start drumming. Breathe out. Feel better.

It's all on me now.

Enjoy it.

TWELVE

The Drumbeat

Our season could end right here, on any pitch. A walk, a hit, or an error and it's over. Or get Ernie out and we survive to play another inning.

Everything's quiet as I throw my last warm-up pitches. Griffin gives me a thumbs-up. Tells the umpire I'm ready.

Ernie steps in. Everybody's yelling again. It's just noise. I focus.

My first pitch is high and outside. *Settle down.*

Now a fastball. Straight and true. Ernie meets it solidly, and I gulp as it flies down the line. Lamar chases it to the fence, and it drifts foul.

"Straighten it out!" calls the runner on first.

"No batter!" hollers Carlos.

Oh, there's a batter. Best one in the league.

Next pitch is low and inside.

"Ball two!"

Don't be afraid of him. Pitch!

Bam! Another sharp hit, but it's out of bounds.

Ernie runs his hand across his face. Wipes it on his shirt. Stares me down.

The pitch looks good, but the umpire says, "Ball three."

Griffin calls time. He ambles out and flips me the ball. "Don't walk in the winning run," he says. "Make him swing."

My mouth is dry. I look to first base, then third.

Tune it out, Javon.

I throw. Ernie swings.

"Strike three!"

Exhale. Fist pump. Run to the dugout.

"Whoa," Coach says as we jump and holler. "It isn't over yet."

Right. It's still tied. It felt like I just won the series, but all I did was get us out of trouble.

And I'm on deck. I pick up a bat. *Slow down*, I think. *Focus.*

The last few minutes have been a whirlwind. We need a run. I need a hit.

But my thinking changes when our leadoff guy draws a walk. A well-placed bunt will move the man to second, in position to score.

Ernie's still out there. Seventh inning. His pitches haven't slowed. But maybe he's losing control. The first pitch is way outside and it smacks the backstop. Our guy easily makes it to second.

I'm still bunting. Third base is closer to a run than second.

Ernie takes a little of the heat off his pitch, not risking another wild one. I tap it up the first baseline and sprint. Ernie makes the play and throws me out, but I moved the runner to third.

When Carlos walks, the Turnips' coach finally pulls Ernie from the mound. He threw a lot of pitches. We all clap for him. He shifts to shortstop.

The new guy is sharp. Three straight strikes.

Lamar steps up with two outs. We are so close to grabbing the lead!

"Redemption, Lamar!" I call. We fought all the way back from that three-run deficit. Now he can give us the lead.

"Strike one!"

I send him a brain wave: *Ignore it. Just hit.*

"Strike two!"

I grip the chain link fence. Study the pitcher. "Come on, buddy!"

Whack! Ernie leaps for the line drive, but it clears his glove by a foot. A run scores. We got it!

Carlos rounds second, then stumbles. The throw from left field catches him in a rundown. Ernie tags him for the third out.

But we're leading.

This is it.

I grab my glove. The drumbeats start. Griffin puts his hand on my shoulder.

I take a big drink of water and walk to the mound. Three outs from the title.

Throw some easy warm-up pitches. Listen to that beat. One-and-two-and-three-and-four. BOP-bop, BOP-bop, BOP-bop, BOP.

The drums stop. The batter toes the dirt. Griffin signals for a fastball.

Here we go.

Last time I won a championship was nearly three years ago. My YMCA soccer team went undefeated, with Torry scoring most of our goals and Marcus getting the assists. I wasn't much more than a placeholder on that team.

This one's different. I've played a key role all season, and especially today.

"Strike one!"

I hear my dad yell, "Yes!"

Lots of people are yelling, but I hear him clearly. He's usually the quietest guy in the bleachers.

"Strike two!"

Ki and Tavo bang the drums.

Sherie yells, "One more!"

I've watched James and Ernie wilt in the late innings today, unable to throw strikes. But I feel stronger than ever. I've only thrown eight pitches.

Here comes the ninth. It's perfect.

Good-bye, batter!

Griffin fires the ball to James, and they whip it around the horn. One down.

The second batter keeps fouling off my pitches. I throw a few balls.

With the count full, Griffin signals for a change-up. But the batter knocks it up the middle for a single.

"Let's turn two!" Carlos hollers.

But I walk the next batter.

Griffin trots out. "You with me?" he asks.

I nod. He turns and gets back behind the plate.

"Any base!" James cries.

"Strike one!"

I like that sound.

This batter is tall. He has a big strike zone. He also has power, so I can't give him anything meaty. Keep it low.

"Strike two!" I can feel the wind from that swing. If he had connected, we'd be done.

My hand's a little sweaty. The ball slips as I throw it, and the batter has to jump back to avoid getting hit.

I wipe my palm on my knee.

Pressure. Let it go. Big breath.

"Strike three!"

BOP-bop, BOP-bop, BOP-bop, BOP.

I feel another surge. Rear back and spin the ball as hard as I can.

It skids in the dirt and bounces to the fence. Griffin pounces on it in a second, but both runners advance.

Second and third. A single will drive them both home.

Coach stays in the dugout. Griffin doesn't say a word. It's all on me, and I know it.

The batter swings hard at my next pitch. He misses.

I let out my breath. Two more. One at a time.

Fastball. Straight down the middle.

He bunts it!

The base runners are sprinting. I charge toward the ball, scoop it up, and toss it toward Griffin in a single motion. He catches it with his bare hand and lunges toward the sliding runner.

There's a hesitation. Then the umpire swings his thumb. "Out!"

We won!

I flop onto the mound and stare at the sky. My teammates lift me up. Griffin grabs my cap and waves it in the air.

The drumming is more intense now. Lamar, James, and Carlos start dancing. Griffin peels off his catcher's mask. He's dancing, too!

I climb the bleachers to Ki and his friends and bump fists with them all. Ki hugs me and tells me I was awesome.

"Nice touch with the drums," I say. "Helped me keep my head on straight."

"That's the idea," he replies. "Focus like an eagle. No distractions."

I sit and listen as they keep playing. My teammates are still on the field, hopping up and down, wrestling. The Turnips are watching from their dugout, waiting for the presentation of the trophies.

"Get down there, brother," Ki says. "Drink it all in. Victories are fleeting. Enjoy it while you can."

I walk slowly back to the field. Ki's right. Before I know it this game will be a memory. We'll move on to another sport.

But I'm taking some things with me that count more than any win. Confidence. Progress.

And a drumbeat I'll carry forever.